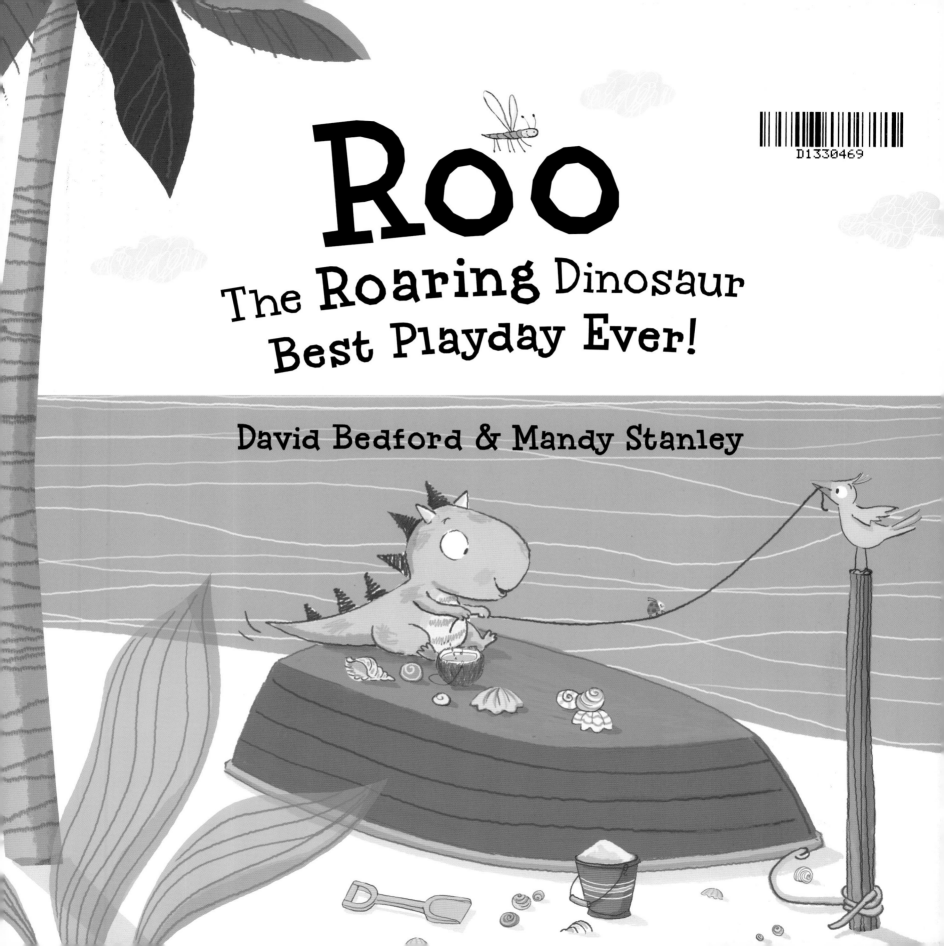

Roo

The Roaring Dinosaur
Best Playday Ever!

David Bedford & Mandy Stanley

Roo the Roaring Dinosaur
lived in a little dinosaur house on
a little dinosaur island.

It was
Roo's home!

Wooly

Every morning Roo **hopped** out to play.

Today Roo decided to go . . .

that way!

SEA

Off he sped on his scooter.

Wheee!

He **splished** and **splashed**
along the hot, sandy beach.

Then Roo dug deep holes
and piled up the sand to make . . .

'Sand Roo!'

said Roo.

Just as he finished . . .

. . . he heard rustling
in the trees.

Somebody
was there!

'Roo hide!'
he said.

'Boo!' said Roo, bravely.

'Hello!' said the
new creature, who
was big, fluffy and
very friendly.

'I'm Erik. I'm so glad I
found your island, Roo.

This map showed
me the way.'

'Can I sit down?' said Erik.
And he sat on the Sand Roo!

'Ooooops,'
said Erik.

Erik Island

'Sorry, I'm always doing things like that.'

Erik didn't mean to be clumsy, so Roo took him along the beach, splishing and splashing.

'Ooops!'
said Erik.

They **jumped** through a sparkling waterfall.

'Ooops!'
said Erik.

Roo decided to take Erik somewhere a little less wet.

Roo showed Erik how to swing round and round a tree.

'Ooops!'
said Erik.

At last they climbed the
steep steps to the top
of the old volcano.

'Wow,' said Erik.
'I can see all of your
island from here.'

When Roo looked too,
he saw something he
had never seen before.

'That's my ice ship,'
said Erik, proudly.

Then he gasped.

'OH NO!
It's melting!'

Roo and Erik scrambled
down to the seashore.

Roo jumped into
his little boat . . .

. . . and soon towed the ice ship away from the hot beach and out to sea.

But now there was almost **nothing** left of the ice ship!

Erik looked very worried. 'Can I get in with you, Roo?' he said.

Roo wasn't sure if he wanted Erik in his boat.
Erik was always breaking things.
He might break Roo's little boat, too.

'Please!' called Erik from
his little bit of ice.

'I'll be very
careful! I promise!'

So Roo made a **brave** decision.

'Erik, jump!' he said.

Then . . .

'ROOOOO!'
roared Roo in surprise.

Erik rowed and rowed
and **rowed**. Roo's little boat
had never gone so fast!

And in hardly any time at all . . .

Erik had rowed **home!**

'Stay for tea,' said Erik.

'I bet you've never played in the snow before.'

Roo liked snow.
He dug deep holes
and made . . .

'Snow Erik!'

said Roo.

Then they sat together and shared
sips of steaming hot chocolate, and watched
bright night colours swirling and dancing
and bursting in the sky.

But when Erik went to make more hot chocolate. Roo began to shiver.

Erik's island was far too cold for a little dinosaur.

It was time for Roo to go home.

'Here,' said Erik. 'Take the map, it'll help you to . . .

Oh no!

I've ripped it in two!'

'Ooops!' said Roo. Erik and Roo giggled and giggled.

Roo rowed back across the
big waves. He thought of Erik's
strong paws pulling on the oars.

And he rowed and rowed
and **rowed**, and in hardly
any time at all . . .

Roo was **home!**

'Roooo!' he roared as
he raced along on his scooter.

'Hoooo!' he sang
as he sprang into his little
dinosaur house,
and . . .

'Roo-hoo!' he smiled, thinking about his funny new friend and the **best playday ever.**

Erik Island

The End